Watermarked

A Poetry Collection

....

Cynthia James

ISBN: 978-0-9936094-0-4

For information for permission to reproduce selections from
this book, email Cynthia James at
james.cynthia@gmail.com

Visit Website: www.cynthia-james.org

Cover Design and Photograph by Cynthia James

*Some of the poems in this collection have appeared online
in slightly different form on Geoffrey Philp's blog
and in Small Axe's sx-salon*

For John

You were more storm-tossed than I could even fathom;

self-consumed, I fell asleep

much later to find you'd disappeared beneath the waves

when I wasn't looking

Table of Contents

Proem – Learning to Swim

1. Signs and Signatures

2. Parchment

...

Preface

Beginning life in a new country is an act of faith, but as exciting and as full of promise, as it is, it is also undoubtedly traumatic. Indeed, given the harsh economic climate at the beginning of this 21st century, to trade the cocoon of the familiar for the hoar-frost of the unfamiliar by choice, can be considered foolhardy. Such uprooting may even be unnecessary, since hopping on a plane, tweeting, skyping or googling interconnects most worlds.

After all, for the hyphenated Caribbean citizen, these are not the *Empire Windrush* days of almost impossible return through the Atlantic passage via the Bermuda triangle by boat to one or other designated mother country. So what regressive mentality could cause a liberated Trinidadian female in this day and age to return willingly to swear allegiance to her Majesty the Queen?

Watermarked is a dialogue that engages this as one of its questions. It is a watershed sustained by a cyclical confluence of answers to why people leave, what they carry, what they bring, what they expect, what imprisons them, and what anchors they find to fashion their continuity.

For instance, one of the signs that never fails to catch my attention whenever I ride the underground Toronto TTC, is the almost overlooked warning to passengers to "mind the gap" on alighting and disembarking at stations. I like to think that *Watermarked* minds the gap - the gap between past and present on which futures depend.

And so, *Watermarked* is in essence a migration poem that develops in four exploratory progressions:

Section 1: Signs and Signatures searches for new bearings.

Section 2: Parchment revaluates indelible referential frescos.

Section 3: Reversing Falls listens to and learns from other travellers: for the seas of adventure and shipwreck belong to no one.

Section 4: Google Knows Your Name affirms one's inconspicuous, yet distinguishable omnipresence in the schematics of the universe.

The collection opens with a proem, "Learning to Swim," and ends with a postscript, "Runway," intimating the high-stakes and the double-consciousness involved in taking-off and landing.

In fact, the open-ended flux between the pages of *Watermarked* suggests the impossibility of relinquishing any of the identities one acquires in a lifetime. What struck me most in the retrospective revising and reordering of this collection was how much re-village-ization it contains. On reading or on hearing these poems read, people have often asked whether I am Haitian, Cameroonian, Ugandan, Somali, Jamaican, Ghanaian. What presumption does this hold about culture and identity; about nation and nation-language; about archival presence; about who I am, who I was, and who I am becoming?

Geoffrey Philp's blog-spot, in particular, his Poetry Fridays, became a buoy for the first sightings of some of the poems in *Watermarked*. I first met Geoffrey Philp at the Caribbean Writers Institute held, to the great alarm of many in its early years, north of the geographic Caribbean at The University of Miami. Then as now Geoffrey's creative talent, conviviality and generosity have remained firm anchors for me as for countless others. I know in some respects I have let him down. But One Love, Brother, One Love.

Cynthia James

January 2014

Proem

Learning to Swim
(Taking Basket)

Dive down and touch the bottom with your palm,

the silver piscine boy said, *Like this -*

then head between his arms, fell forward

tall, with such amazing grace and form,

and when he rose, pupils glossing the coffle of beginners

scoffed, *Your turn, Bermuda Girl,*

whoever heard of an islander that cannot swim?

She an inland girl, come high and dry across the sky,

bread on salt cod, shipped and dried

for generations from his here new found land.

Imprinting on the deck a rocking hold, thighs trembling,

she fell forward, head between her arms;

the wretched chlorine stung her eyes;

blinded, she touched the bottom with her palm

and lungs bursting, rose in his blue pool gasping

1. Signs and Signatures

I want to be as happy

as the 4-picture-portholed people

on the cover of this newcomers' guide:

an olive man, son high upon his back,

an Afro-ed woman, uniformed, white womb around her neck,

two construction hard-hats, one pink, one white,

and a couple representing all of Asia, indexing an iphone and an ipad.

All are fair and smiling.

Which one is me?

I'd like to smile back,

my hand creeps up my cheek,

Am I smiling?

Against the sky, flames sabre-toothéd

a watermarked red flag

Dentonia

Maybe I'll learn to love here where

they don't know a cold Carib is to die for;

where people don't love like in a brighter sun

    -    those they love 'beat under love'

        and love to death themselves and those they love -

it's June; the stone- washed denim sky's the same,

roiled at cuffs; eyelet holed skyscrapers stand

tall, stick men wearing dark shades in the evening

sun beyond the baseball red brick diamond;

but a couple kissing in a street of riot

deepens faith in love amid a city's loss;

here in Dentonia, too, among the astral yellow dandelion

weeds: for just as many spent, a cloudy intertwining helix

spiked and seamed with DNA disperses promise

for the bissextile and even the year after:

an eternity of love. Yet flame-torched eyelids

travelling slits, singed plucked chicken,

bare of all fine hairs and yellow skin, stand guard,

slumber-less; willing out sizzle and spit -

coz every time he comes, my Saga Boy, his smile deflowers;

even when he unscrews the can, his bitch, Tan-Tan can't even run;

Don't light me up again ... Please ... Please...

... aspergillum splash ... match scratch ... Boom!

-    yolk ringed in white lace bubbles rippling in a pan of butter

flesh pumiced in heavy metal acid wash –

yet in this refuge far removed from Mango Bascapool, Doux Doux

Darling, and YES! Tabanca, love perchance again will come

in this white desert, this weedy astral dandelion patch,

eyes wide open in a whirlpool haze of summer

amid shade trees I cannot name nor claim,

(but does that really matter?)

On Other Continents

you guys are mixed, he said:

mixed with what, I said; obviously

he'd read my claim: divided to the vein;

où avez-vous appris le français?

Back home, I said: in a convent: You?

Welcome Brother, long have I sought you –

Arrivants: we kiss cheeks masked the same,

set to scavenge slim phenotypic spoils

who would sell the other first -

a sail is a sale is yet a dirty *sale*

this vast value village's cold -

though self-exiled we still need muffs, boots,

Joseph's coats, no frills - food: basics;

our curse's genesis is close yet distant -

quintessentially human, recurrently man-made

Buxton Lady Under Lock Down

we'd sit in the elephant ear of a marble queen,

icing dusting the skylight, listening to the wattle

wheezing through the atrium, the karaoke

tinkle of Old Virginny, Old Kentucky Home inside

warm apple cider drunk, she'd say, "Those songs

we learnt in school, is only when I come I understand.

But I is from Kaywana stock; this place make you

more black. Bring me some cocoa butter

when you come next time," she says, rubbing Buxton spice;

we watched cars swish, slip, slurp past grey-fingered trees;

"Was a day like this that send me here; white, no headlights;

I didn't see, nobody see, nobody say, nobody talk for me; he

burn like crisp; if wasn't for my Buxton pride I dead already."

But summer she was different; then we went out on Wheel-Trans.

"Look," she says, "Imagine me who make with nail, tinin

and hammer, grater, from scratch, buying coconut in frozen

quarter-pound square pack. You know bout metamgee?

conkie? A tumbler of swank, Man, down the hatch!"

Then we would join the ladies for a round of bingo,

even take in the fashion show. "Is a man you know!

Wait till she start to strip. We ask the recreation people

for him every year." And she shouting loud, "Go more!

Take off the shirt!" And bad talk Victor, her one and only son,

full of guile who just so, she-say-he-say, "Let's go for a drive ..."

but she going back for her gold ring on the bureau

the Deceased Egbert give her. Now that was man!

"I could teach you the computer; you'd like Facebook,"

"Unh-unh," she said, "is a long long way to Tipperary.

Dawg a lay down, ashes cold."

Sunday Friends

On this ill May day trestles are laid, sausages split and sizzle,

there is bread, baked beans and Quiche Lorraine,

faith, hope and charity displayed;

but stick a pin -

my grief's chaptered in the pages of the ages,

anthologized, googly-fied on countless web pages,

put to bed; we're safe

"Come sit with us," they say, and let me listen to them talk,

offer more bread, more sausage; "Eat," they say; pressing

a doggie bag when I'm full; "Or we'll have to throw it out."

to them I'm either a gang-raped Rwandan, an

earthquake Haitian or a refugee Côte D'Ivoirian.

My specifics, the backseat crush of a Curepe PH- taxi

in the ripening armpit of a macomère; what's the difference?

My Monday-Wednesday-Friday friends

work irregular hours; Sundays on Sundays off;

shifters scanning subway schedules strapped to poles:

weather watchers, PSW day/night-care givers,

an open Bible here, Asian or Arabic hieroglyphics there,

 "It's cold today!" "Did the 23 go up?"

"I just missed it; the driver saw me but he didn't stop."

Or else silence ...

i-Pod mantras stream through womb-shaped wires

avoiding common words in this tired old experience;

a stilted ESL confounds what we wouldn't

know how to, or are too afraid to say;

so on this ill May Day I break bread with Sunday friends

I pray with, sing with, laugh with, even trust enough to tell my sins

but stick a pin -

for the Knights of Columbus have set the tables

my servers, their sisters, the charitable daughters of Isabelle:

my great- great- great- grandmother must be turning in her grave.

City Beautiful
for CWSI 1992, Coral Gables

she wasn't there the day before,

and then there she was, buttressed up,

green hair, grey keloids girdled up her trunk.

People walked wide, giving alien berth

transplanted Solitaire; could scarce forbear

to breed from seed or sapling anymore.

Five days out, her green hair dried,

old scars thickened into footholds

her elongated phloem engined up, amphibious.

Her skirting slacked - and soon everyone forgot,

or so it seemed, for none can say precisely

when her trusses loosened

but she took root like an institution

prickly proud, bearing bunches of red berries,

gri-gri, just like that girl lounging

in the fingered sun-slats of her fronds

Toronto ESL

(Bill K.)

see how as you begin to speak he swivels slightly,

leaning back, black boot-tip pushing forth a stylish

kick below his full length dry-cleaned knife-edge,

hands pocketed, head forward, blunt, so you've become

the bottom of his perpendicular, he right-angled

to decipher the surround-sound whirling at his outer ear

       (once it was so simple!

             a ripple lent quaint ambiance to dinner dusk

                at Queen's Quay, or Spadina)

so many mangled vowels now do confound;

moving mumbo jumbo; no-speaky-English?

the onus put on you, since reading liver-coloured lips

and midnight stroma evoke a trick-or-treat recall;

so you balance backward, by a hair, to soften

the opaque amber offered in his cochlea

Cutting Lent

We'd cut lent, little finger hooked like chain link,

talk for-fended; and if you couldn't or forgot

to hold it in, you'd face the consequences

mouth open, jackass jawbone dropping,

better say it safe, unsaid in the roaming mind,

self-witness only to itself, than witless in the wind

one day respite, thank St. Joseph; but if you were really good,

you did the whole forty days, Palm Sunday, Passion Week,

waited for the hot cross buns and image of a ship-shape forming

on the hot stone of a cracked Good Friday egg. But first you had
                              to hang

Shrove Tuesday's clang of cowbells on a crossed stave; and then
                              the ashes.

New dispensation; carne vale; that long time Lent is here again.

Christmas Flash Mob

so they lit the third candle, the rose among the mauve,

a half-split caimite really, the plum gradating

to a fuschia, vulva-centred, fleshy white,

a moist black star buried in every quadrant whorl

but no witness to this story to fill its many gaps:

how a girl hearing voices that she pregnant

(second hand), just ups and take a journey

to a distant land to visit an old cousin by herself,

that a baby leaping in a womb confirm; they say

she end up staying with the cousin three months

and the cousin husband, old Mahal, you know Mahal,

revving car and turning corner, with bubbling lip and foot and hand;

he doubt; they light a candle on his head; strike him dumb;

and Shadrack, too, for years we live with Shadrack,

walking up and down with rope, brown gown and Jesus-

sandals clanging bell, a dead ringer for the same John

so I'm telling Bev about this flash mob, livening the humdrum,

this Sunday stir up, twelve-eleven; people in their dan-dan!

Everybody singing: *Exultez de joie, acclamez votre roi!*

led by a doe-eyed angry man playing an organ

and I say: We just practising to maim and kill tomorrow

the only way we know how. See those stalks clawing

the promised fire at the centre of the ash-coal dawn?

See how right now we longing for the white stuff?

All this, One cycle, One répétition. Near Easter, we

cursing that same white stuff: White Stuff, Be gone!

And my daughter ups and say: You know you! You'd better

keep your mouth shut! Your great grandmother shut her mouth

so you could born. You always jeopardizing things, opening

up your big mouth. But I tell her: No worries, this poem not

getting print no how. Is just you know how sometimes when

you're breathing and you notice that you're breathing, just so you start to gasp because you cannot find your rhythm? Well

the half-split caimite's just a figment of that Carib woman

far from home, dreaming a slice-a black cake, a slice-a

Scrunter pork and a drink a ponche à crème! Ah! to top it off

Janus
for Clement

You stand just beyond the doorway

flattening dough from palm to palm,

teaching me in solfège the second part

of Rock of Ages; fire on top, fire below,

the bake cooks and we sup

later the darkness deepens,

in your tender care I rest,

and when the daylight fills the sky

and all things bright and beautiful

ah! we venture out again.

When I complained,

"Just draw the milk,

not count the cows," you used to sing,

Hymns Ancient and Modern,

as caution and refrain.

So when doubt comes colder than this minus twelve,

tin graters shred the quick and sting,

green hidden okra silk pricks skin,

breadfruit drips milk blistering,

farine from twisted cloth comes crumbling

this is not nostalgia, this is what I am -

the yam vine curling on the prop,

carailli, cane, and cow-heel soup -

walking these amazing highways

way beyond the 49th parallel.

So as I hurry in this chill to dedicate

this New Year, Father, when we meet

I know not how I will explain:

two generations after came bearing greetings,

the younger, plugged in, head bobbing, multitasking -

leave him: his father says: he says

he is agnostic - why didn't I press,

what did I fear, when slipped I farther

and left them grinning at *How I met*

Your Mother and *Two-and-a-Half Men?*

2. Parchment

Simple Private Things

simple private things no one would guess

like learning the week's hymns through earphones pressed,

or finding natural air conditioned peace

distilling through your branches and your leaves;

listening to raucous children swinging

back and forth, skied higher than the soaring,

swooping seagulls, now digging in the grass

for earthworms wriggling as their die is cast.

It's June, water spouts abate the heatwave,

but August comes soon heralding your grave.

How you do face defeat, return to dare!

Watching you every year helps me to bear

blind hope that spring will come and with it rain,

the will to rise from death and death again

for even when tornado bullies come,

wrenching your arm, cracking your shoulder from

its joint, threatening your years with sagas grim

such that chain saws need amputate some limb,

sap flows, you mourn but these ordeals surmount;

what's left, tallied, you take into account

and cap with green sleeves, sprouts covering scars,

calling to fete a medley of guitars,

Come Sparrows, Come Finches, Come Warblers! Cheer!

Soon no one thinks you're any worse for wear.

How even through cold fingers, gaunt and grey ˙

you manage to display the Milky Way!

an overarching sight none can explain -

like dove returning, twig in beak again

Red Revolution Cover Girl

In those days galvanize was painted green

and terror came through static air, well...

not as pranks, but as sirens. The fight back then

being against TB (not BC), there were nine of us

between breastfeeds; a love child - 2 girls 2 boys,

4 times each, as if my mother's eggs had planned

us playmates, twins not being in his or her genes.

We played around our cauldrons stoked

with charcoal bones burnt in the earth.

And sometimes there were white wisps

far out against the mountains. I pointed,

but she didn't look. "Eat. Don't talk,"

my mother said, caulking my mouth

with finger-softened potage.

We weren't allowed to light the sky,

not even with our shouts or cries;

and so to pass the time we often counted Xs

on our Bingo stack hanging in the kitchen,

11 cards in our stack; and every week

Father brought them back with 11 more

Xs. "Don't play with those," my mother said

as she put away our rations. Then one

ordinary day he came red can a-swinging,

changed to overalls and cap, and leaning

a ladder to our roof went up; came down

cap, face, and overalls blood-splattered.

I knew I shouldn't, but since he didn't often smile, I asked.

He raised the clotted brush, and quick-daubed my nose!

"What are you doing?" Mother said,

so he advanced to daub her too.

She ran back into the kitchen.

We laughed, and when our tag was spent,

he put the brush to soak in turpentine.

My nostrils twitch still at that polish scent,

Red Revolution Cover Girl!

Calypso Love

she was always on her feet; she suffer

from insomnia, so she'd wait until

the son-of-a-bitch start to doze off, until

he nearly sleeping; and standing far she'd

poke him with the long handle of a cobweb

broom as soon as his body start to slacken.

Get up, get up! You can't rest here. This is not

a hotel! You can't eat here and sleep here

on my strength, and afterwards dress up in clothes

I wash to go and meet your Madam!

Meanwhile she have a pot of water singing

on the stove as back up to douse him with

from far. Coz after all, is only so much

disgrace woman can take. But one time

he attacked; she didn't see it coming;

a tumbling and a rumbling and a

BOOM BOOM BOOM; a grunting,

then a quiet. Nine months later

I had a baby brother. And my father?

She love him long and she love him strong -

which stand me in good stead, coz

when my turn come, I had it down cork,

the alpha and omega, chapter and verse,

of how to make love, and how to take love

Portraits
for Bev

... and if you're lucky you'll have time

to give her treasures you'd really like to keep,

candid shots you didn't have time to stick,

stuffed in the crevice of an old album:

grandmother louped - at whose wedding?

pixelated father - flying roof-high, dancing the cocoa,

dingy-white sail-shirt, sole umbra in candescent sky;

except ... what if you're not so lucky?

And she arrives to find you toying with your rat-pack,

walks over for the spot Alzheimer's check,

watching bony fingers braille-ing faces.

"Who's that?" she says -

you swallow to suppress the croak,

lest whisper uncontrolled, segue into

"Mum, you must be tired, you need to close up."

Old fish head, grey rim around your iris widening

you who once sucked fish eye lenses, biting down

white archived print, flattening celluloid images -

you need her help to extend this raw slide

view of still live images, 'Sable Venus', 'Flagellation of a female

Samboe slave', loin-clothed, gift-wrapped

at wrist, flayed flailing - Jesus! crucified,

beatified, mummy-fied in plaster of Paris,

exhibits all, all these too captured silent.

Madras

(on viewing Delacroix's The Women of Algiers)

I'd recognize that madras anywhere

just as a nuzzling newborn knows the nipple from the womb;

the distance between maiden and handmaid's light as lace,

splotched as the white bodice mothballed in a wispy camphor moon

in that olive garden

pearlescent ring, slave band, earring

balance light and dark, motion and stillness;

crosswise, a strip of caramel on chocolate grips,

tapes and measures straddling hip;

winged talons flèche the yam lift of her instep -

palatial slavery entrusted to the back-glance of a slave girl four women, and a hookah,

(one a servant girl), console a third;

the red light window in the antechamber composes

sprawl, entwining tenderfoot – arm, leg and haunch,

butterscotch their Queen Anne cabriole.

But mirror, mirror on the wall, gilt peep, a Tom!

a serpent's slid behind the tease of drape about to fall

sole witness, bone-white lambskin

ॐ hanging on the front wall -

this recognition prescient as a caul,

blindsided by the hauteur of a servant girl

Shadow

The day the pastor brought him, between howdyes

a flash leapt out; my eyes and ears caught just

a rustle: tall razor grass straw closing back across

the graveled cul-de-sac. Might deter snakes and rats,

the pastor said, and thieves from coming up the track

until more people buy more housing lots and turn

this part of Cleaver Woods into a real development.

Morning and evening I put out discarded pots,

rinsed, not washed - one food, one water,

burnt fare and crusts thrown out on to

the concrete landing next to the building tap.

In time I learned to occupy myself, not wait and watch.

In time I saw him – slinky brown, just like the colour

of this fall jacket - under the eaves, far, but close enough.

And sometimes stooped behind the landing door,

noiseless, close enough to smell, to touch, I'd

give a million dollars to know what he thought,

save for the door, a single heart between us.

By day, ears pointed up, angled at the cul-de-sac,

he ate, tongue barely touching, water slopping;

and in the time I took to recognize the sigh

across the way was nothing but the wind's loud

yawning, he'd disappeared when I'd looked back.

An offside route back into the bushes?

But by night, monarch, crouched lion-like,

ruffles of his wimple, silver-flecked, soft-pleated

shawl, from neck past shoulders resting lightly

over haunches, fixated on each sway and parting

of the cul-de-sac, I watched him from the cracked

door of my landing: Rat free, snake free, thief free,

at least I could return the favour. Could he not hear

one heart pulse the intervening quiet? Just One?

My noose comes up; two silver slits shoot up;

in the open, falling over upturned crocks,

heart bursting, flailing, tugging, trailing rope

clattering, receding through the gravel, gone!

Days pass, by and by I perk up, scouring the cul-de-sac.

Dumb beast! Strangled, snarled? The rope snagged?

I wake up sweating just before bared ivories sink into my palm.

No, your Shadow's different; same dun colouring,

but apart from that ...

just give him time, he'll come back

He Used To Close His Eyes

He used to close his eyes,

go deaf and blind and immobile

save for the yellow miniature clutched

joint phalange to breaking point, tight

within his palm, curled lashes winking;

lips clenched, tight, so tight, not answering

"Jay, we're here," cooed soft and sweet,

in birthday party, Silver Diner Nickelodeon –

the Mummy-Yummy! put-on voice,

spooned squash planed-in-from-sky voice,

(knowing you and I wouldn't be caught alive

with that horrid health inside our mouths);

so you would have to lift him out, leading

in a blind man's bluff across the street,

his knuckles bent, still so tightly gripping

his yellow mini Matchbox.

You didn't even wave, look back ...

how my chest heaved and shuddered

long after bawl and kick and snot dried up,

while older druggies penned-up watched

my senseless scrap with socialization;

hours passed: hands up - hands out - hands down,

story, recess, heads-down-on-desk after lunch,

until dread turned into ritualization.

His day too shall pass,

remembered dryly as those

'bad-old-days' or 'good-old-days'

those astonishing proverbial ways -

SPARE THE ROD and

MANNERS MAKETH MAN -

hard pen-knib grip and inkwell dip,

exacting hundreds of calligraphic cursives.

Extending my cracked knuckles now,

bent, ruler-crabbed, arthritic, I wonder yet,

What if they didn't nearly break my hand?

Would I have learnt: BLESSED ARE THE MEEK!

(love-abuse so narrowly limned,

caressing these senescent limbs),

SPEECH still considered SILVER

SILENCE still forever GOLDEN

The Subject Line

for Catherine

Make sure, I say, quite deadpan on the first day,

to put your name and ID number in the subject

line, watching for first fractious signs; and I may

or may not add, depending on a cough, a sigh:

Not my responsibility if your email goes to SPAM;

and if still no FUCK anonymous floats by on thin ice,

I might chance: And no sugardaddy/sugarmommy@hotmail.com.

Act-like-the-professionals-you've-signed-up-to-become.

But you never know, this might not be a spineless bunch,

so if things look a wee bit dicey, I switch quickly to icebreaker mode

and go for groups; it sets them talking; student input always works,

set Alex and his seatmate Alice customizing our contract:

> Before you start your homework feed the dog
>
> No more than two grandmas allowed
>
> No headphones – let lecture in, and lecture out

(Sick kids carry karma, so most likely they'll skip that one).

Let them have the upper hand out-monstering the monster

in this poker we're both experts at. But remember,

always cap *Welcome to College 101*, if winter, with

the March-Break-in-Cancun-no-Extensions sermon.

So there I am, two months later, screening -

sleepers, skippers; texters, taunters,

wide-legged drifters, trousers barely covering their crack,

habituated subjects, simple past, past perfect, conditionals,

when C and D rise upper case 'tween lower case before my eyes.

Seriously? You who know where barley grow, going for a second

chance, single mother, pre-teen kids, never missed a class?

Only to descry the-powers-that-be had huffed your subject line.

You no longer owned it, the typescript peaked and valleyed

did indite, stark, on open sheet-shroud, formless white.

Charcoal Monochrome

July first, 10 pm, rumblings, flashes, fireworks:

You'd think that three years on, the smell of maple wood

and honey smoke would lift the downward spiral

not provoke the cock-set cough of burning black sage,

coalpot centred, bedroom closed to smoke the mosquitoes out first;

not evoke West Indian Reader nights

playing picture or no picture on a perwinkled door stoop,

page opening by chance on Hugh Cameron's A Lonely Life -

a wizened woman cradling scant firewood

panier bare, selvedge sere,

explosion of her blood red shawl, sole highlight

against pink pigeon-breasted crepuscule

not invoke in the gloaming, yawning kitchen window propped

half-staff, pearly prism-ed light transmuting inner *lepais* thatch

from Scot to classic Boscoe Holder still life painting:

- jug-eared coalpot, brimmed; blunt quartz of coal;

- corkscrewed gazette paper; ash-fuzzed nickeled cleaver;

- pointy shards of tinder; curled peelings of cassava

- pewter pitcher, hornéd spout; silver halo, condensed milk
                              tin-cup;

- speckled mortar, granite pestle leaning like a dislocated
                              thumb;

- rugged torchon, grits of sand cresting stilt-legged washstand

- villi-feathered sooty corners, clamber-spidered V-greased gutters;

- and soft limned mid-height above, a double-breasted dove-grey

- form, fingers pouched; mouth smudged with itty-bitty edge of
                              coal

You'd think by now I'dve dipped and done my genuflection,

lightened gilt greys, contrite, confessed and done my penance;

(Will you think of me, and love me | As you did once long ago)

Perhaps next year, my 4th year, when palm shells race up the sky,

to rocket trunks with bursts of coconuts, my chants will be as loud,

transposing old anthems with new chromatic metronomes

Lorem Ipsum

one arch and bald, describes it: *palpable and mute,*

in a lightning flash another calls it out:

Be Black! Spoken silently or loud.

How the dickens do they know your words' worth?

Pound out your dos and don'ts,

and if at times they're difficult to discern,

try chiselling gently, perhaps

they're already configured on a Grecian urn;

touch-type and watch the nonsense script peel back,

it's your own lorem ipsum, your dream weaver.

Whatever you do, for good or evil,

avoid the absolute place-holding wrap, for

-WYSIWYG, WYSIWYG, WYSIWYG-

Cicero always has the last laugh.

3. Reversing Falls

How I Spent My August Holidays

i

imps and sprites weave in and out of spouting sprays,

cascading crystals slap the dais, a cerulean fake lake,

guardians' eyes half-closed keep watch in sprawling shade,

migratory seagulls squat nearby like giant button mushrooms

island-accented children zoom in and out pulsating jets, vacationing

a life time away from Plaisance, high-stepping over fowl shit,

squealing when thunderbolts hit, setting out from Grandma's cottage

to see the Godineau come down, awed by fallen trees, crop damage

come September, (hopefully) they can now write 'one bright summer

day', that mocked cliché, and not be shamed into tearing out

the page, to begin again in regulation local colour:

'How I spent my August holidays'.

ii

So why you leave? And don't give me to hold story bout

the stifling Creole and the shirt-jacked toad, so many women

burnt! how you was so-o-o tired: after you went so public

(nobody ask you!) and make a pledge, Iere, my Love.

When in the shimmering cascade in the laniappe parade,

a girl wine-ing to the side, duck out the spray, slink off the dais,

turn right on Canton, left on Paul, cross the EMR,

pass Miss Mongolas, the dasheen ravine, Ramkelawan

trace, dew still snot-ing the blue-flower water grass

down to the yellow filament, snaking the edge of the pitch;

crunching gravel like golden Demerara, going to keep company

with Dolores for the day; she not talking, so I have nothing to say.

iii

She's the ghost in the choir, recessed on the low riser,

aloft in the right corner, watching intercessors,

veiled Marys mewing at weeping candles, waxing,

waning, even before their backs turn, learning:

> how to ride a donkey with a belly sideways
>
> how to trek to the well, as long as it takes
>
> how to raise a child that you can't control
>
> how to walk with company albeit alone

asking Cecelia in the stained glass a favour, begging

a flame; knocking three mea culpa-s on the washboard

of her frame; descending to meet the matriarchs face to face,

only to discover her face and theirs are one and the same.

iv

This is neither the beginning nor the end,

just a turning of the page, ask Kincaid,

Zuela unveiled chapter by chapter, *madras entier.*

tèt anlè, foulard, chimiz, jip, broderie anglaise

so you try to explain:

> *One* - that you ent gone nowhere

> *Two* - that you is still you

> *Three* - that you ent kill priest

so why a girl can't decide how to spend her August holidays?

The Sugar Clock

This setting back and forwarding

the clock, lengthening and shortening time,

is not in my experience.

I learned and laboured under one timepiece,

the sugar clock, somewhere near the great house

deep in the crevice of my ear still going strong

the wailing ICTA horn, blaring five to seven, five to twelve

and five to four o'clock; more than a century of wailing,

usine - plantation time seems O so distant!

when to pick up tools and lay them down and when to lunch -

I have no picture of this timepiece, no sense of what it was,

but in the bowel of the you-we sugar factory, sure it was!

Some say 'twas pressured steam, but in my mind it was a round

alarm with finger-lever, iron, brass or shiny silver, nippled like

the cycle bell Works' workers rode out, clicking after it went off.

Who pulled it? Or was it automatic?

Did its wail wind round the campus weekends, too, when I was gone?

Or did absentee hands run round its face invisibly

like on these fancy modern digitals?

Halfway between a warning and rebellion

sometimes it sounded like a conch! but no, it was no conch,

or else I'd seen a Maroon man, Orisha Andrew?

master drummer, going in and out.

I moved in step with it, shell shocked.

Who turned it off? And when?

Did its sly slumbering regime rankle you-we historians?

Who knows the what and why, the grip of memory?

Oriens Ex Occidente Lux

Did it shut off on its accord when the steam engine rusted? When did

it cease to be that relic of 'the bulwark that we watch' way south?

Wayward

If on a winter's night you meet me in a tempest,

the smell of squid upon my breath, the sea for an urn,

recalling Noah, Jonah, Ahab, the twelve million drawn,

the leapers from Sauteurs, the Zong, the coffled

Henriette Marie, and no less the Lucky Dragon,

me, Ryou-Un Maru, Fishing Luck, flying Dutchman,

(over three thousand still missing from that flood),

note well, it all comes down to liquid balance.

You saw my masthead raised to sky,

praise staggering to Haida Gwaii

as I edged closer magnified, portholed

in the crosshairs of binoculars.

Mice and men ringed round the world,

Prosperos, big and small, at safe distance

called, "Clear and present danger. No treasure.

Perchance some artifact is found, send but that caché back."

Blasted, barnacles and all, torpedoed,

they watched me fall, laniards taut,

dead-eyes shrouded, a requiem on every news.

Pacific, with amazing grace, I went down

smoking. So you with glittering eyes scuttle along!

Out gunwales of glass-bottomed yachts, on

clear days, don't come snorkelling these burial

grounds, frolicking among my pumice stones.

And, *if on a winter's night* you meet me in a tempest,

different name, different place, my vast

endeavour submerged in the ocean for an urn,

(no more than a pipsqueak on a pequod,

to Prosperos of every port, mere casualty insurance,

underwritten, one side profit, one side loss),

note, mice and men may scuttle my nightmares,

but never reap the harvest of my dreams.

The Beaches
for Lennox Brown

Yet another Kew Gardens behind this groyne of beach,

a queen, a king, a union, further down, a Kensington -

salvages, this anomie for replicas, selections of empires,

Stonehenges, Tajmahals, recurrent Chinatowns.

The fronting lake grins and bears accumulating silt,

suppurating, giving grudgingly to those who

on a dying evening come to pace this boardwalk,

then go inland to lay down shield and sword

facing the convergence of millennial waters from all the cardinals,

even the brutal baptisms of line-crossings way down south; who come

not to judge the grey man kissing the green woman (not his wife);

nor Mary, hair let down, bra loose, bridge in hand, resting her gums

nor sniff the trailing whiff accusing the teenagers, nor

notice the men in black with walkie-talkies cycling by,

but leaving Leuty and the dog run, pass the gaping bandstand,

trail fingers over commemorative plaque, wondering

who's the dark child in the drinking fountain and where's the Native;

smell the white hyacinth perfuming the round Gardener's Cottage,

swallow the saliva accreting in the throat gland, conflicted,

awed at the power of salvages to unify yet nullify

but super-glad to see you in the missed of this, walking briskly

round Queen's Park on the cycle track, up near Kilarney

just before you take the Y on Maraval; and I hail you out,

Lennox! Come leh we go down Macqueripe and buss a lime!

and you jump in and we heading for a real salt-water bath;

going past the tall blue Guardian Spirit with the silver wand,

on this make-believe beach, boardwalk, in these Q-Gardens,

Magnificent Seven in the distance, we the only salvages in a different
place and time

Noah

I.   The Flood

It's June, the sun is fire bright, no rain, but

dark clouds way up north, zigzagged with yellow

loud POTOWs like fakes in comic books;

the Oropuche, fat, brown and silent, not its usual

crawfish trickle rushes through the diamond lattice

lacing the bridge's silver derricks, snaking within

La Vega RC, leaving a cake of mud behind,

mocking the children's hurricane warning:

> *June too soon*
> *July stand by*

And for the first time in twelve leap years,

he'll not be there beyond the bamboo patch,

shoots trailing in brown water, faking death,

surrendering to the inundation, racing for

the reaches of his cocoa, coffee, orange tract;

but even before that, flooding his stilted ark,

where he will not be to secure these,

deserted since his passing:

II.   Living-Room

A copper-toned Atalanta in plumbago auriculata,

life-sized, one sandal lightly laced, slightly heeled,

steps out her frame, one foot in front the other,

laconic sliver of a silver smile unfurled over her scroll,

Indian inked in Olde English, sprung in a loose burnt curl.

Adjacent, a father's life-sized aeneid moulded in passe-partout,

a scrawl of collegial witnesses for endorsing footnote – these two

portraits, sole lares and penates on these sepia-coloured walls

III.   Dining-Table

this pock-marked altar of endeavour, pleasure - cedar

Queen Anne, stump-calved, bow-legged from waist down;

a homework table, chess and checkers table, christening table

overlaid on Sundays with white crocheted pineapple spines,

covering a brother's Marvel kingdom, frustrated pen-knib

digs,and countless circle and triangle dark spots, once hot

from pressing irons, scorching stove-to-table pots

now cold, felted with a bristle of white tufts

eating's been a challenge here: royal settings come

in sixes − six chairs, six plates, six teacups saucers,

for a family rhythm-ed to nine by natural childbirth.

Invent more seats and feeding's yet a tangle;

fruit, passion spills among a maze of elbows,

a baby trills golden pumpkin fed in four-finger shovelfuls;

overhead, pitch pine creaks - not damp, not termites,

but resin bladders fattening by day, and flattening by night

IV.   Master Bedroom

red, green and blue-striped ticking, bare of counterpane,
hills and dales and fibrous thorns, centering a despond of tears,
abiding trinity still tucked in one corner of the bed-head frame
        - black and gold King James, beribboned green, purple, red
        - copper crucifix, bent knee and head, stigmata verdigris jewelled
        - white exhausted candle, blackened wick, wept crust of prayers
chrome ghosts bouncing off city cars race the full-length mirror,
dust mites on the armoire play checkers with chipped porcelain

V.   Tool room

two-door steel chest, stilt steps recessed;

stone-bitten blades' glint barely light their contents,

so pull the fly-strip dangling at the forehead:

> burnished calf-skin poniard sheaths, brass-stippled cutlass
> handles peep; spirit level, shaving plane; saw, hammer, trowel,
> fork, hand rake; pickaxe, shovel, swiper, hoe; louchette to
> hook and jab pods of cocoa; retracting tape, bag-twined stake,
> cleft with a cocoa needle like a G-stave; cured crook stick,
> bass broom, crocus bags; coiled hose, tall rubber boots, spray
> cans; wheelbarrow caked with concrete mix; on shelves
> around, slat nursery boxes; seed packs, mauve, yellow,
> saffron, green - cabbage, pumpkin, aubergine; and too, his
> beloved hardy blooms: periwinkle, canna, and marigold

VI.   Chicken Coop

rusted hasp and staple, caws;

face height the Coleman mantle purrs;

russet hens on damp sawdust

poke forward flat yellow glistening ovals;

he pegs his lantern to a 12-inch nail, cups one by one,

and shaft and shard clipped back, lifts each above

the snakes and rats, flailing through mesh wide enough;

the man pulls a plank between this vermin and his chickens

VII.   A Moil Of Spores

and looking around before going up, picks up

the broken toilet seat, bobbing to the front in all that

brown Oropouche coming down, though in this high June

not a raindrop. This Noah man in fig-stained shirt, knowing

all can't be saved of all this stuff - three bags of cement,

the top one gashed; cracked corn, the remnants of a weeviled sack;

piles of tiles, the surplus from the bathroom job; a cocoyea broom,

orange fibre tufts cosy-ing up for once to Jack Spaniard honeycombs.

A sunbeam augurs this moil of spores:

Your father work so hard, she says, *and all of allyuh leave and gone ...*

Amphibian

On bat-blind nights brown figure-eights flew in,

groundnuts, tops and bottoms well-developed

soft-bellied, pincer-headed with a tease of wings

(a cross between a scorpion and a cockroach),

seeking the light, but not gaining height, plopping

in her wild-hair thicket, burrowing, hollowing,

cold, aiming for her camouflage of scalp.

In daylight, examining their handiwork, limp

stalks, the colour of Saskatchewan potash,

fingering his loss, her father called, "Go, get

the carbolic soap in the blue enamel cup,"

(shaved and swirled to milky suds); then

dress band trailing, she walked the kitchen plot,

flicking four-finger cupfuls, for the family was organic.

To her delight scorpion-headed nuts rose up,

bobbing, wobbling, wriggling in the scorch,

racing for the safe hillock of her instep

that turned and crushed them in their tracks.

Much later, the hotplate sky cooled ring by ring

to night-black iron, treachery long forgotten,

she sprawled like a limbo dancer, rose

mango cheek, ripe juicy slice in glow

of flambeau, hanging from the crossbeam.

Meanwhile the backdoor sea scoured the beach,

swallowing fallen hog plums, balatas and wild almonds.

At its touch she shot up! leaping on the tabletop,

screaming, flicking wildly, ghosts rising

from the shadowed séance circling thick beyond.

.

Frenzied and on lurching feet,

drums ricochet through her small body.

Dislodged, the scorpion-headed nut

lands with a thwack on the floor. "Look,

it's no longer there!" her father says.

But feet tucked up off where it's disappeared,

she still flicks in fits her crawling hair.

Even later still, chancing on a split clothes-clip,

caught in a clutch of cobweb, rugged scrub-

board, midriff clenched, missing its metal

corkscrew hinge, she fondles her find

crisply encased in spidered white, when

sharp feelered splints dry prick her quick.

She'd picked it up, touched it! Caressed it!

Freaked out, she flicks the fallen mummy

across the floorboard crevices into the open.

Much later still, five thousand miles from home,

lifting limp stalks, up bobs this nut-brown figure

eight, top and bottom well-developed,

among roots she'd newly planted.

She knew they crawled, jumped, ran and flew.

She hadn't realised they could also swim.

Malpeque

the tide was out, the sea had disappeared,

so I could walk far out the ocean floor,

sand-scouring two equal halves of shell

to make a pair of earrings, two matching cups,

keepsakes, flesh-coloured on the inside,

shaped by what they once held.

No need to dig, these chip-chip were on the surface, dead;

but so many of the outstanding were unhinged,

and even those un-afflicted in the head were badly

frayed, battered, left behind in the spume's wake –

some big, some small, not text-book pretty, but different -

Ask Rihanna … all cut along the selvedge

some bronzed, some bevelled, some striated,

some the colour of donkey-eyes,

some fat and black like Orinoco sea coconuts,

some pale, transparent, shaped like Douens' hats,

some like hanging fingernails, white chips from an enamel posy,

(dented just at the upturned lip, near the curved ear-grip) –

yet all heirlooms, antiques, unusual;

Balandra whiff, curry-chip-chip, steamed

down in coconut milk, a blade of stinging nettle

(chardon béni); on top - a blood orange scotch bonnet.

Vat 19! Something to "Awake the Spirit!"

You'd know it when you saw it.

And many seemed to have it -

these clutches of Malpeque shells picked up,

right side to find a matching left side,

fine Muscovado clawed all up under my finger nails;

and the further out, the more bosey I got, until

I heard something like a conch blast and looked back.

So far I'd come, and no exact match,

nothing whole, nothing that made sense.

I'd never pondered much before on mounds I had despoiled;

tide in - tide out, facing the Atlantic chip-chip was always there.

Now just a clutter in my hand of so-called good halves -

Drop everything? Go back? But go back where?

Lucy Poem

Follow the rope past the hair-wreath in the parlour,

Home Sweet Home, Bible, Queen Anne side dresser,

past the horsehair's pretense of wealth

in Anne's room:

the cast iron bed

the cross-legged nightstand

the pitcher and wash basin

wallpaper of climbing roses

the brown puffed-sleeved gloria dress

the shutter's open, Dawn Treader,

how's this different from the life you've lived?

in the yard:

the ox-drawn dray

for the horse-drawn carriage,

corkscrew croton for the black-eyed susan,

snow queen hibiscus, red folding umbrellas

hanging over the white picket fence

the sun flares,

the subject reflects

down the steep slatted terrace:

a tonca bean grove,

no crisp curled birch,

no Lake of Shining Waters,

but a Dragon and a Serpent - a Mouth,

beyond the Haunted Wood Trail

toggle shutter and aperture -

reciprocity and exposure link these continental shelves

Meeting Cousins in New Brunswick

Fake loyalists met us at King's Landing,

Farmer Johns, broad-brimmed, straw-hatted,

in dark-suits with sorrel satchels,

beyond the schoolhouse near

the water far from the theatre where

they practised their transplanted scripts.

Chantwells led through cedar trails,

past water wheel, oxen plough, one solitary molten

ingot, gleaming in a smithy strung with tongs.

Long-sleeved women in frilled bonnets,

long aprons skirted with deep pockets, stoked

tin ovens, tending simple apple pie and homemade bread

clunked water pumps in stove-piped kitchens,

soldered on to cooper barrels, tongues of silver

slithering up the town that drowned -

a real Tourist Annie masquerade,

without the ass and bosom stuffing

of our pillowed Dame Lorraines.

We even tried hand carding fleece,

but left dimpled Rumple to her fly-wheel,

to rove and spin her own yarn.

Boarding our coach for the Atlantic, in time

we left our straw men; one tipped, the other,

hat in hand, crossed his breast and nodded

but on headcount two Trini hogshead were found missing -

No one had seen them since the landing.

Water more than flour! Panic spread,

ending deep in the dark hole of The King's Head -

There they were! Feat had not failed them.

There they were! Old talking and knocking back strong spirits!

Chocolate River

From time to time we came upon caked Vs,

raw creamy clay, fudge-textured, scored

as if raked over with a fork, moist, but

no water bladders springing from the pores;

our tirade spent, the coach was numb;

to compensate for circumventing Fundy Bay,

our guide was heading straight for the tidal bore

Miss Katwaroo's eyes were shut from spite,

"Maracas have stronger Magnetic Hill.

That's what they call Reversing Falls?

Water making giddy round ghost paper mill!"

She'd pursed her mouth, turned key and locked it with her fingertips;

a lace of light and shadow fretted her eyelids,

cold fat jiggling in her jaw to bumps the coach dived in

now and then, we brushed an overhang,

kicking loose asphalt inches shy of precipices;

each clump of bush the same, boiled-egg eyes darting;

save for loose baggage clinking in the overheads,

you could stick a pin. "Mommy, we're lost!"

Miss Katwaroo's lizard eyes flicked open;

the catholic across the aisle rattled her rose petals from Jerusalem

the coach continued ploughing hill and dale,

glimpses of shed snakeskin waiting to be refilled

splayed open between the bushes,

sometimes along the trail, annatto red,

sometimes a sambo-mixed-with-quadroon shade ahead,

sometimes a languid length of ribbon

littering the bottom of the precipice.

And just like that

we fall into a bag of bois flot!

the child's cry winds down like a sugar horn,

lights flicker in the cabin,

GPS and smart phones blip,

flash scrambled AC-DC messages,

blank out, fall dead

the coach begins to tilt,

we're leaving heaven, teetering downhill;

then there it is, the creamy chocolate milkshake

sleuthing towards the Fundy Trail up the clearing,

beneath sun-silvered trees, glinting, quiet -

the twice diurnal orgiastic bore

pictured on postcards we'd bought at Hopewell

men, women, children talk in tongues,

their wonderment to see the Peticodiac swell

under Roy's Accompong thick maroon coverage,

syrup rolling forward, a slight shimmer at its edges

engorging fissures, crevices, distending runnels,

there was no stopping it;

the brown leviathan was approaching.

A wooded track,

flatlands,

some bouncing backseat gripping,

a lodge,

a landing,

and our whole cabin starts to clap as when

Air Jamaica touch down after that long tense vacuum of hovering

Back with the Johnsons

she doesn't see my grey, my ropey sagging jaw,

my pair of crabbed phalanges next to her own;

last lasting image, a crown of orange blossoms,

lace, a fifty metre guipure train, snow white, waving

happily ever after; that's it: for her there is no sequel;

after all, I didn't go off with Tom Thumb or Bluebeard;

so though our macular degenerative gaze wanders sixty seasons

plus, over sun and moon and rain, and for me, hail, she says,

"You're young," though we're both back with the Johnson's;

the fifteen years between us and my flower power

dustings make no difference at this stage; and talk now

as we never could into the lengthening of the day.

(They've plaited us in neat plots; they shake their heads

and wink. They're not so far over the hill that they can't

visit now and then, but thus far they haven't come to stay.)

4. Google Knows Your Name

Keeping Score

(EIIR Diamond Jubilee)

the Bangladeshi boys running between the wickets,

organic bin upwind, recycle bin downwind,

don't know how much we have in common.

I stop to watch them. The bowler sets his field,

comes bearing down, merino whistling,

fielders close in, the batsman pucks,

Kanhai collects his own ball.

An honour guard of Bengal Tiger lilies

edges the path close to their makeshift pitch;

I walk and smile to think now in my diamond jubilee,

my son says to his mates, "Come meet my queen."

If only he knew over the past 60 years

how much has changed from London calling

Constantine-George-Headley-Worrell-Walcott-Weeks

Beginner, Kitch, the run on to the field at Lord's.

Relator warned; then after tea, bad light,

stumps drawn, came the call to rally round;

small island pride seemed rudderless

and Blue Boy signalled for Lara to surpass Lloyd,

but time's a bad night watchman;

that didn't stop the slide for long.

T-20 tweets replace transistor static

chirping in broad daylight down Frederick Street;

Sunil rides with Kolkata Knights and Bravo, Chennai Super Kings.

If, like me, you've got a fair knock,

from time to time you'll sadden at this secret exit dismount classic,

but as you pass through honour guards of red striped canna lilies,

wherever you are, raise a glass to your queen!

Cosmic Molasses
for Stokley

Horn chile,

the limer on the corner blew on a furl,

crushing mica on the pavement, tapping

PRO-Keds a mere mockery of a b-boy move.

The young woman walked on without misstep.

The baby, faced behind on the mother's shoulder,

bobbing, sloe-eyed the four youth on the culvert,

the first interesting sight to light her eyes

since the walk; the curl of honey-spittle dripping

from her bottom lip like an elastic band, snapped.

This house lizard need some sunning;

here, take this flannel ball and go play hopscotch

on the front walk, but stay within my eyesight.

Disingenuous to pretend today I didn't understand;

after all, it was the time of Medgar Evers, Snick

To Kill a Mocking Bird cliffhangers stoked

one after another on the Civil Rights timeline;

sepia-toned, wedge-wood medallion, great-grand-daughter

of a stolen princess and a drunk madman with marble eyes,

(so the nansi story goes), is to play with inside ghosts outside

puzzles forever breaking on the rainbow of conception;

these goddamn particles, however much you think you know,

the sex, the weight, the curve beyond the pulsing ultra

sound, the known unknown, continuing to mesmerize.

The Sun Catcher

When they enter

their eyes will go straight up the pre-shine

dark, and for a moment they will hesitate

before the scarlet carpet once proscribed,

but brave hearted, they'll tramp up the nave

and from the concave chancel

scrutinize amid shadowed burnished pine,

the new sun catchers of Attawapiskat;

Easter moon balms,

one little, two little, three little,

stained glass window patterns,

scored and shattered,

soldered, silver

foiled and fluxed,

simple artifacts:

A for Arctic, B for Beaver, C for Crocodile.

And I, Warahoon, too, will be there.

I'll strike my chest and hope

before the incense rises

they will understand,

this fancy masque I play, this sun dance -

stamping round in circle, low,

hatchet, wampum, Mohawk, wigwam,

feathers trailing down my back,

hand sewn half moons, dazzling

mirrors on my leather vest

and white pants, striped -

is one of my nation's treasures,

(though what I know is second hand,

picked up from a man called horse),

a kind-a *ci-mi-di-mi* really

to dispel a kindred disappearance

Google Knows Your Name

the day, the time, down to the millisecond

stippled in the edges, cropped and tagged

within cascading frames; sized, resized,

three-sixty street-view customized,

one can even put a coloured pegman on her trail,

so what's her story?

since Google knows her name

5:25 pm freeze-frame:

red Toronto Sun, blue Star,

free employment, rent dispenser,

hoity-toity pewter trash-bin birds on wire shit on,

Beck and Co-op cabs lane-centred,

padlocked gate, a woman at the crossroads,

crosses from Sacred Heart to Luke's United Way.

5:35 pm freeze-frame:

there she is again, same white-scarved

bundled female shape, tan fringe-hooded,

street car passing, facing down the far pathway.

The walking, counting led-man knows her;

pin-holed mid-stride, he strides, she strides

across the intersection that way

5:45 pm freeze-frame:

set the yellow pegman on her,

hyper-visualize her game –

high banked snow, tooth-ploughed cobble,

praying-mantis-squirrel, black;

HERBARIUM -

She waits …

5: 55 pm freeze-frame:

white-scarved, hooded, bundled shape

can be deceiving; same as in the first frame -

red Toronto Sun, blue Star,

free employment, rent dispenser,

hoity-toity pewter trash-bin birds on wire shit on,

across from Luke's United Way, Sacred Heart, a padlocked gate.

An Easter egg is hidden somewhere

in these interlocked freeze frames

All Saints - November 2011

(causa latet vis est notissima — Ovid
the cause is hidden, but its force is very well known)

My Dear GPS

You've asked me to confirm; thus I assure

the tremors you experience underground

are not the elephants of Hannibal, nor is

Vesuvius the cause. The cacophony awakening

Hades, I'm afraid, and Charon's frequent trips

across the Styx have quite a different source.

The old girl's quiescent these past sixty-seven

years. Nonetheless, bombs and fire flashes rain

from up above with pulverizing might, such that

Lower Sirtis mirrors the Pompeii we last saw.

Myriad Homeric and Virgilian versions abound,

but, My Honourable Uncle, since you ask:

Alas! Priam and Hector again were cornered;

the rebels and the rabble, both triumph claim;

but all that's certain (perhaps not in dis-order)

is that both were dragged through the streets;

then slain; then photographed for posterity with

V-signs. There were long lines, rejoicing, wide acclaim.

I saw the golden gun;

I heard the berried W-A-A-W;

viewer caution was advised, but old voyeur of our

munera, I watched it all on HD and in 3-D, I might add,

(complicit, some opine, oblivious of our tradition)

from a distance like in that old Gold-Midler song.

But that's old news in the coliseum -

just like these that I'll be brief about:

Carthage and Alexandria still under siege;

sorry for so long a letter, but an earthquake

also shook a pilate's podium while he washed

his hands; in Otta-war as the broadcasters say,

a bunch of crazy people last month chanted

"Arrest George Bush"; serpentine floods

challenge the promise given Noah, wash away

Thailand and Guatemala; even in Paradise,

all man and woman under heavy manners –

curfew in their tail for more than six months.

Yet take comfort; the legacy of Caesar, perhaps

a little rattled, nonetheless, remains intact.

This letter pales compared with multifarious

more illustrious troubadour accounts;

but rest assured, you can depend on me,

My Venerable Uncle, there's more to come

Farewell

P

24 hrs 2 Guinea

the rosewood dawn recedes, thin laced with

milk-heart signatures; the ice below thaws;

brown strangled tufts raise pickanini heads

in cracks of sidewalks

bees are not yet out, but ants climb up and down

viburnum stalks (flush now with scented clusters

where scarce a month ago this sweet lime hedge

was briar patched with thorns)

shivering white petals, antennae digging deep down

in the calyx, feeler-ing the nippled berries hardening

at the cup; it's Saturday, mid-May exactly

and all is good.

At Broadview where I board, the streetcar driver leaps out

to single-point a crowbar switch, the witch-broom trailing,

pulling us suspended on the centre rail, backwards

to Main from Carlton

and I go past the diasporic new-world United Nations

line-up, urging cringing baby bok choy, Ch-u-ut!

to stand up to the threatening fangs

of blood red dragon fruit

at little India, watch the wind float the sari

of the woman with the nakpul and the red dot,

ripple damask drapes and Himalayan pelts

without a touch

glide over earthen jugs, brass vases, shiny cooking pots,

guarded slant-eyed by smiling amulets of Kali, Shakti, Durga,

juggling creation and destruction in multiples of even hands;

mid-May exactly, a Saturday

and all is quiet;

but time is a chameleon, every so often confounding near and distant;

today I'm the Guinea woman, flying three, four, five hundred years,

reeled back before my time across the skein of difference

a frothy wake of spume

dribbling down my chin like soap suds, splashed up from Monday

morning white clothes wash, spores popping as the scum dries,

under the dingy ochred outer circle of a cappuchino sky.

We've run off track

without point-catch in a modern city mapped on ancient legends;

a heart shakes off its smouldering ash, and there's Akan Oroonoko,

trussed up like a suckling pig, puffing pipe, taunting his tormentors

eyes kindle hard-stare accusation;

otherwise, sudoku and the 24-hour paper occupy; meanwhile

brown babies nonchalantly chatter, mocking this old street car,

pulling me, Guinea woman, back to a different place and time

1000 Words

for Anson

when you sent from Wales those thousand words, in three unlit
cupcakes, all the way,

three candles, a bedside monitor, white sheets, a loving wife and you
in dark shades,

was it a challenge from the poet master? What were you really trying
to say?

I smelt hops bread, saw Boboy on Sapphire Drive eating a cheese
soufflé,

St. George's, Royal Victoria, 6ᵗʰ Form, You-We, New Voices – light
and dark charades,

when you sent from Wales those thousand words, in three unlit
cupcakes, all the way

Sadhu of Couva in a cloud of light and sound, mouth rounded in an
ॐ, pray

tell, O Chela, the vanity of counting age reduced to symbol across
decades,

was it a challenge from the poet master? What were you really trying
to say?

a plastic container's just a tray; the one behind the camera and the
one in front display

the gap between the fleeting and enduring - love lived and practised
never fades;

when you sent from Wales those thousand words, three unlit
cupcakes, all the way

I understand the why of Chepstow, your visit with the Normans, the
proseleelas, Hey

Alfie! the distant Lovesong of Boysie B.; but the nansi of that emailed
photo yet evades;

was it a challenge from the poet master? What were you really trying
to say?

Poet Laureate, no offence intended, just two meagre heartfelt words -
Happy Birthday!

And yes! Rage. Play your ace of spades! Be not gentle with the horseman.
Send him back to Hades!

When you sent from Wales those thousand words, in three unlit
cupcakes, all the way,

was it a challenge from the poet master? What were you really trying
to say?

May Shuttlecock

The day before, I'd left the gold leaf candelabras in Cantaro;

white holy ghosts wing-spanned the high blue apse of Santa Cruz;

I was confirmed again, crowned with cascading tulle, wild lilies

and forget-me-nots. 'Twas May, the rains had not yet

washed away the yellow candles kindling tender fires,

and surfeited, I wondered how and why I'd sunk so low

within the vale to miss the Hubble view and give this up.

The old singer in the corner needed but a shuttle;

I went out and bought, passing the day soft, loud

pedalling the treadle's lockstitch revolutions.

The next day my flight confirmed, I climbed the clouds,

suction-cupped my ears, swore against all birds, and landed

routinely at Pearson. By evening I'd trod fallen acacia crisps,

windblown bread crumbs, and yellow buttons helix-spiked,

kicking heads sprung in thawed and tilled dogs pats.

For the Survivors

(Personally, I concluded that no place in the world was entirely safe for an African, and that for many of us, survival depended on perpetual migration. Aminata Diallo –Lawrence Hill: The Book of Negroes)

I looked for you tonight

but the green icon next to

your name remained greyed out

I just wanted to link my breath

with yours across these portals

the ancestors float, back and forth

invisible, to say

that there must be some reason,

in spite of bad experience

we ceaselessly confront

all warning not to trust large bodies of water,

wandering the world on the meal ticket of our brains

in peace, to say

that I no longer shield my eyes

from those I meet in glove-worn bus stops

searching baleful pools,

wondering over fretted cheekbones

if the same pass brought us to this searing cold.

What have we come to see?

(some neither refugee nor out of poverty),

begging pardon each from each?

to learn the secrets

of the Olmec fathers? to trace the flame

of their endeavour to out-know the beyond?

I'll look for you again tonight

just to tell you not to worry, I have plenty company,

I'm good and will be - zaboca grow in plenty country

my navel string done bury, so

I seizing my freedom by any means necessary, and to remind you

to bring the black bag, the keys, and the tokens when you coming

What Makes You Feel That I Grieve Less?

when winged black stealths with yellow

bat-pricked eyes shroud my skies?

What makes you feel that I don't tremble

when my buildings flame and crumble,

when my people even without wax

and feathers try to fly, wishing just

to see the dazzle of the light, spirits

soaring in the open for the last time

The whole world comes to see and taste

the wrack and good of your big apple.

Names roll by, three thousand, more,

I didn't know but miss; they were

my hope and my example. What gives

you provenance on grief? Through my blood,

pain pulses likewise like a gushing fountain

over one and other, yet another

three thousand -- mine, yours, ours.

Will you come to my memorial? Or just

shout "Sacrilege," from your pedestal?

Writing Home

Hold nothing against the daffodil,

potent against the cancer of self-love and aged forgetfulness;

but beware the bulb; mistake it not for the onion;

it can kill; it's subtext for the Ides of March, but also

'comes before the swallow dares' in *The Winter's Tale*;

grind and smear it on topical wounds only;

for it's death and spring, bad luck and morning glory;

it flowered in the Garden of Gethsemane and at Stonehenge;

meanwhile turn the page; it's the only way to complete

your chapter of the story, you Mau-Mau-ed, castrated,

you waiting for the return of the Balangiga and the Kohinoor;

the eye of history is more distant than you can imagine;

learn the lore of all bush medicine with thanksgiving;

go where you will, love where you will, live where you will

Postscript

Runway

so I had done it, the injured thing my heart

had dreamt at four, at eight and later on,

perhaps at twelve, at thirty, forty-five; and now

at sixty, the air bag pressed into my chest,

inflating, no more room, I wedged out

the scene was just as I had pictured it:

cat's eye radials, headlights, orbs,

inflected pyramids, torch-beam mirrors:

self-pity's promise, red-riding peace; beyond

snow bank, wilderness, avalanche, freefall

still, it's good to know escape is not just a far-off drone,

a child's sky-wave, berth unknown, unburdened ache of bone.

Walking up the cottage stoop, I wring my wrist full circle,

and going in at All Days Three, lower the burnt-down wick

on smoky lamp-lit yellow, ribbonned Home Sweet Home

Other Books by Cynthia James

Novels:

Sapodilla Terrace (2006)
Bluejean – A Novel (2000)

Narrative History:

*The Maroon Narrative: Caribbean Literature in English
Across Boundaries, Ethnicities and Centuries* (2000)

Poetry:

La Vega (1995)
Vigil (1995)
Iere, My Love (1990)

Short Stories:

Soothe me, Music, Soothe Me (1990)

www.ingramcontent.com/pod-product-compliance
Lightning Source LLC
Chambersburg PA
CBHW060642130626
46555CB00002B/925